Contents

Chapter 1
Serious Magic

"Mia's doing it again," said Billy in a whisper.

Juno was painting her nails. "Mia's doing what?" she asked. She didn't look up.

"*Wishing*," said Billy.

Juno looked over at Mia. "How can you tell? She's just looking out of the window."

"Her eyes are closed," Billy pointed out.

Juno went back to her nails. "She's probably just thinking."

"She's wishing. I can *feel* it," Billy insisted.

Juno rolled her eyes. "And what does wishing *feel* like when it's at home?"

Billy fiddled with the sparkly little stud in his ear – the one he insisted was a diamond. "When it doesn't work, wishing feels sort of *sad*."

"Mia's sad if she still thinks wishes come true," Juno said under her breath.

Mia couldn't hear their whispers. Her face was pale and her eyes were shut tight as she wished the same wish over and over. But when she opened her eyes, nothing had changed. She was still in Mrs Turvey's messy sitting room. She was still a foster kid. She could have cried.

Then she saw Billy and Juno watching her and gave a little gasp. She'd been wishing so hard, she hadn't heard them come in.

"Were you wishing you could go to the ball, Cinders?" Juno jeered at her.

Billy shook his head. "She was wishing that she could live happily ever after, weren't you, Mia?"

Mia's eyes went wide with shock. "How did you know?"

Billy gave her a sad smile. "*Everyone* at Mrs Turvey's wants to live happily ever after."

Mia didn't know what to say. She'd been living in the same house as Juno and Billy since the start of the summer holidays. But she didn't *know* them. She didn't *want* to know them. Since she had come to live at Mrs Turvey's, she'd felt like she was in the wrong story, a story with no happy ending. She wanted to find her way back to the *right* story, the one where her mum came back from the hospital and Mia got her real life back. Juno and the other kids were all part of the story that Mia was trying to escape.

Juno stretched out her hand to admire her shiny silver nails. "I'm guessing your Happy Ever After wish didn't work out then," she said. "Seeing as you're still here."

Mia's eyes filled with angry tears. Wishing had been the only thing she had left. It had been her secret. "It didn't work because I'm *stupid*, because magic isn't even *real!*" she shouted, and then she started to cry.

Juno gave her a funny little smile. "Maybe you just aren't doing it right."

"I – I don't know what you mean," Mia stammered.

Juno folded her arms. "Maybe everything isn't about *you!*" she said. "Maybe Billy here would like to live happily ever after, did you ever think of that? Maybe you're not supposed to hog all the magic for yourself."

Mia had to blink away her tears. "I didn't *mean* to hog the magic."

"Sure you did!" Juno said with a scowl. "You think me and Billy are, like, these tragic *loser* kids that magic is too good for!"

Mia went bright red then because Juno was right. That was *exactly* what she'd thought. When Mia had wished to live happily ever after, she had only thought about herself. She was so ashamed she didn't know where to look.

For a long moment, nobody spoke. One of Mrs Turvey's cats strolled in and started to rub against Billy's legs. Mia stroked the cat so she didn't have to look at Juno.

Then all at once a wonderful idea popped into Mia's head. "Juno, what if we all wished *together*?" she asked.

Billy looked impressed. "*Three* people wishing! That's *serious* magic!"

Juno never ever looked impressed. She shrugged. "But what if I want something different?"

"We're just wishing to be happy. The *magic* decides how we get it!" Mia explained.

Juno thought for a minute, then she grinned. "OK. But don't try to make me hold hands."

Mia giggled. "You don't have to hold hands! We'll all close our eyes and I'll say the wish out loud. I'm going to wish for everyone at Mrs Turvey's."

Billy's eyes flew open. "Not Kyle?" he asked in dismay. "Kyle is really mean!"

"We've just been *into* that, Billy. Like you said, *everybody* wants to live happily ever. We can't leave people out," said Juno, closing her eyes.

"This time we've got to wish for everybody, even Kyle," Mia agreed.

For the first time in months, Mia felt happy and hopeful. Wishing had felt like such a lonely thing to do when you did it all by yourself. But three kids, joining their wishes together? That felt like serious magic, like Billy said!

She shut her eyes and said their wish out loud. "Please let every single person at Mrs Turvey's live happily ever after! Now you've got to wish so hard you see stars!" she told the others.

Juno gave a little gasp. "I can see stars already."

"*And* me," said Billy astonished.

Mia saw them too. Tiny gold stars dancing behind her closed eyelids.

A warm breeze began to blow in through the window.

It smelled like sunshine and roses and foreign spices.

"Mia, we did it *right*! It's *working*," Billy whispered.

They opened their eyes. And then the magic began.

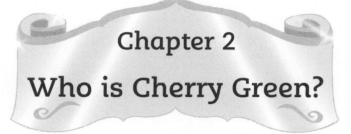

Chapter 2
Who is Cherry Green?

It didn't seem like magic at first. They just heard a creak as Mrs Turvey's gate swung open. Juno looked disappointed. "It's just another foster kid."

A girl was walking up the path. She had long, curly, black hair and honey-coloured skin. Nobody was with her. No social worker. Nobody.

"If she's a foster kid, where's her stuff?" Mia asked.

The girl didn't have any luggage, just a colourful patchwork bag over her arm. As she passed the window, she looked up and gave them a cheeky little wave.

'It's like she knows us already!' Mia thought.

"She's not a foster kid. She's magic," Billy said with total confidence.

The doorbell rang and they heard voices. Mrs Turvey was laughing. "Just ignore the dog! Come in and meet the others."

They looked at each other, amazed. A strange girl had turned up by herself and Mrs Turvey just let her in, chatting and joking as if they were old friends!

"I *told* you she was magic," Billy whispered.

Mrs Turvey bustled in. "Juno and Mia, meet Cherry Green! She'll be sharing your room. Cherry, this little scallywag is Billy."

Mia and the others stared at the new girl as if she'd dropped out of the sky. Mia was sure she'd never seen Cherry Green before in her life, yet somehow she felt like she *knew* her.

Cherry had tried to make herself seem normal, Mia thought. She had given herself a normal-sounding name. She was dressed like a normal girl in a denim jacket over shorts and leggings. But like a fairytale princess Cherry had a magic shimmer that she couldn't quite hide. Who *was* this strange new girl? And where had she come from?

"Come on, girls, take Cherry upstairs and make her feel at home," Mrs Turvey said.

"I'll carry her bag," Billy said at once.

Mia and Juno led the way up to the little front bedroom. Billy followed with Cherry's bag, and the dog and the cat followed Billy. Mia had never shared a room with anybody magic before. All of a sudden she felt shy.

"Um, that's your bed by the window." Juno said in a super-polite voice that Mia had never heard till now.

They were all feeling shy, Mia realised. They had made a wish and a strange girl had appeared out of the blue. Now nobody knew how to behave.

"You can use these two drawers if you want to unpack your stuff." Mia's own voice sounded super-polite now, just like Juno's.

Cherry didn't seem shy at all. "One will be fine!" she said, and her voice was natural and friendly like her smile. She unzipped her patchwork bag and took out a small pile of clothes, a toothbrush, a hair brush and a comb.

"Is that all you've got?" Juno was so shocked she forgot to be super-polite.

"I'll only be staying for three nights."
Cherry gave them a funny little smile as if the
four of them shared a secret.

'Will it take three nights to make us happy
ever after?' Mia asked herself, surprised.
She wondered when Cherry was going to say
something about the wish. Maybe she wouldn't
mention it at all? Maybe she'd get straight
down to the magic?

But Cherry seemed perfectly happy just to
hang out with her new friends. She sat down on
the bed. "So how many kids are living here?"

"Six at the moment," said Juno.

Billy ticked off their names on his fingers.
"There's Mia, Juno, me, and Rosie and Riley.
They're twins."

"You forgot Kyle," said Juno.

"I can't *ever* forget Kyle, Juno," Billy said in a tired voice.

"Don't you like him?" asked Cherry.

Billy shook his head. "He's mean and he steals things. You see my stud in my ear? It's a very valuable diamond that my real mum gave me. Kyle said he'd steal it while I was asleep. He said I wouldn't even know he'd done it until I woke up!"

"Kyle stole the only photo I've got of my mum and dad," said Juno.

"I got it back for you, though, didn't I?" Billy said proudly.

Juno nodded. "Mrs Turvey's put it in a safe place. But Kyle says he can find it any time he wants."

Mia expected Cherry to look shocked but she only said, "Let's not worry about Kyle now. Can you pass me my bag, Billy?"

"Isn't it empty?" he asked, surprised.

Cherry shook her head. "I left the most important thing till last."

Cherry lifted out an odd-looking parcel. Most parcels are wrapped in paper but this one was wrapped in an old piece of carpet. The carpet looked incredibly old, but Mia had a feeling it was really precious. The colours glowed like jewels and golden threads glinted among the glowing reds and blues.

They all watched as Cherry carefully opened it and took out what was inside.

"Oh, *what?* It's just an old book!" Billy said in disgust.

Age and sunlight had faded the book to a kind of all-over mud colour. The shabby leather cover was covered with scuffs and scratches. There weren't even any words or pictures on the front to let you know what was inside. Mia thought it looked like something you'd find at the back of a junk shop.

Billy looked deeply disappointed. "I thought it was a magic wand or a sword," he moaned.

"No offence, Cherry, but you should drop that in a skip," Juno said.

Cherry laughed. "This book has been in my family for hundreds of years. Do you think it would still be here if it looked magic on the *outside*?"

"You mean it's really magic?" Billy whispered.

Cherry's dark eyes sparkled. "It's extremely magic! It belonged to my great, great, great auntie. I can never remember exactly how many greats so I just call her my auntie."

"Can we see inside?" Billy begged.

"Just a little peep," Cherry said.

And she opened the book a tiny crack.

A warm breeze sprang up. Mia felt it ruffle her hair. She smelled sunshine and roses and foreign spices. She heard distant voices and laughter.

Then they heard a new and closer sound. Someone was coming up the stairs.

Cherry closed the book with a snap and the sounds and the warm, spicy smells faded away.

"So where is she, then? Where's this new foster kid?" a voice demanded.

Mia gasped. She wanted to tell Cherry to hide her book but it was too late.

Kyle was already standing in the doorway.

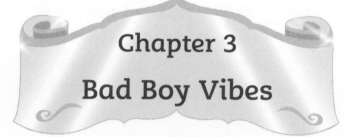

Chapter 3

Bad Boy Vibes

Kyle didn't wait to be invited – he just strolled into their room. His pale green eyes lit up and Mia could see he was on the look-out for trouble. Kyle always had to stir things up, she thought. He couldn't just join in with everyone else. He had to pick a fight, smash something, *nick* something.

"Aren't you going to introduce me to your new friend?" he asked, with a grin at Juno.

"Kyle this is Cherry, Cherry this is Kyle."

Juno said it so fast that Mia knew she was desperate for Kyle to go away. So was Mia. She had a million questions to ask Cherry about her magic book, but she couldn't do it with Kyle listening in.

Only Cherry seemed pleased to see him. "Hi Kyle!" she said, with a friendly smile. Mia was alarmed to see that she didn't even try to hide the book. Cherry didn't know that Kyle's restless green eyes saw *everything*.

Kyle stuck his hands in his pockets. "Must be a bit of a come-down for you, Cherry, to have to live with all us lowlifes," he said.

Cherry picked up her comb and started to comb the tangles out of her long dark hair. "I like it here. It's interesting."

"The only person in this dump who's *interesting* is me," boasted Kyle.

"I don't agree," Cherry said.

Kyle's smile vanished. "You don't agree that I'm interesting? *That's* not very nice, Cherry!"

His voice held a threat but Cherry didn't blink. "No, I do think you're interesting. But Billy and the others are *really* special."

Kyle's face twisted. "Oh, Billy's *special* all right! He's the thickest kid you'll ever meet. Juno only cares about her looks. And Mia thinks she's too good to breathe the same air as the rest of us! Wait till you've been here as long as I have, Cherry. Then we'll see if you still think they're all so *special*." And he stormed out of the room.

"People always say I'm thick," Billy said in a hurt voice. He put his arms round Mrs Turvey's dog and hid his face so no one could see him cry.

"Kyle will have it in for you now," Juno told Cherry. "You'd better be careful."

Cherry was the only person in the room who didn't seem upset. She just smiled at Juno. "We're not going to worry about Kyle, remember? I like your nails, Juno. Will you paint mine silver like yours?"

Juno looked surprised but pleased. "Sure!"

Billy sniffed back his tears. "I'll get the nail polish," he offered.

Mia went to stare out of the window. She couldn't stop thinking about Kyle's cruel comments. She'd only included Kyle in their wish because Juno had accused Mia of hogging all the magic for herself. So Mia had wished for happy endings for *everybody*, even mean, spiteful Kyle. Now she thought she'd made a big mistake.

The kitchen door opened downstairs. "Tea's ready in five minutes!" Mrs Turvey called.

"Quick, wave your hands around! Your nails are still wet!" Juno told Cherry in a panic.

"You mean like this?" Cherry started to flap her hands like crazy.

Mia let out a surprised giggle. Kyle had tried to spoil Cherry's arrival with his bad boy vibes but Cherry hadn't let him. Mia decided that she really liked Cherry. It wasn't just the magic. Cherry was good fun, the kind of girl Mia dreamed of having as her best friend.

Downstairs, the kitchen was full of good cooking smells. The little twins Riley and Rosie were already at the table. They stared at Cherry with big round eyes.

Mrs Turvey carried a huge home-made shepherd's pie to the table. "Now don't go giving yours to the dog," she warned Billy.

Kyle came in late. He didn't talk to anybody, just sat down and started stuffing food into his mouth.

When the meal was over, Cherry went to help Mrs Turvey get the younger ones ready for bed. Juno and Mia had to stack the dishwasher.

"I keep pinching myself in case it's all a dream," Juno whispered.

"Me too," Mia whispered back.

"What do you think is inside her book? I think it's spells."

Mia shook her head. "I'm not sure."

They went upstairs to their room. Cherry had left the book on her pillow. Mia kept catching Juno looking at it. Then Juno would catch Mia looking.

Cherry came in so silently that they didn't know she was there until she spoke.

"It's time," she said. She slipped off her jacket and turned to pick up her book.

Next minute Billy rushed in, wild-eyed. "Kyle's says he's going to do it tonight!"

"*Billy!*" moaned Mia and Juno together.

Cherry shushed them. "What does Kyle say he's going to do?" she asked.

"He's going to wait till I'm asleep, then he's going to nick my diamond! He says he's *really* going to do it this time!"

And Billy started to sob as if his heart would break.

Chapter 4

As Many Stories as Stars in the Sky

Mia jumped with fright as the bedroom door smashed against the wall.

Kyle barged in, talking a mile a minute. "I knew Billy would come in here and blab like a big baby. I was just messing with him, OK? Why would I want a stupid little bit of glass?"

Cherry jumped up and put herself between Kyle and Billy. For the first time Mia saw the T-shirt that had been hidden under her jacket.

It had a message on the front in glittery writing –

Cherry Green, Story Queen.

Kyle saw it too. He gave a jeering laugh. "What's a *story queen* when it's at home?"

"Stick around and you might find out!" Cherry told him.

'No, don't,' Mia thought in dismay.

Kyle was disgusted. "No way!" he said. "Stories are for little kids!"

"My auntie wouldn't agree with you," said Cherry, with her usual friendly smile.

"Your auntie?" Kyle looked blank.

"She was a very famous storyteller," Cherry said. "In fact, it was stories that saved my auntie's life."

Juno's eyes were huge. "How come?"

Cherry puffed out her cheeks. "It's a bit complicated. Basically, my auntie's parents married her to this strange king who had a bad habit of killing his brides on their wedding night."

Juno and Mia gasped.

"To be fair, his first bride did run away, and I think that had made him go a bit crazy," Cherry said.

"I can't believe they still made your auntie *marry* him," said Mia in horror.

Cherry nodded. "I know. Me neither. But she was a clever cookie, and she didn't fancy being another murdered bride. So every night she told the king the longest, most thrilling and most action-packed story she could come up with! Then, when dawn came, my auntie always stopped the story right at the best part. She hoped that the king would be so desperate to hear how it ended that he'd spare her life until the next night."

"Did it work?" Juno asked.

"It worked brilliantly! The king completely stopped being crazy, fell in love with my auntie and they lived happily ever after!"

For some reason, Cherry's words made Kyle angrier than ever. His face twisted up. "Just listen to yourselves! Nobody *ever* lives happily ever after! NOBODY! Get it?" He rushed out of their room, slamming the door on his way out.

Mia didn't really notice. She had been staring at the sparkly message on Cherry's T-shirt and she had suddenly worked something out. She turned to Juno. "It's not spells in Cherry's book. It's stories! That's why she's the story queen!"

Juno stared at her in dismay. "What good are stories? They're no use at all!"

"Stories *are* useful!" Billy said. "Didn't you hear Cherry saying about her auntie and that scary old king?"

But Mia totally understood where Juno was coming from. Stories were all very well but they couldn't change someone's life, or make them live happily ever after. Spells were much better.

"Are your auntie's stories in that book? Those ones she told the king?" Billy asked.

Cherry nodded. "My auntie's stories plus millions more. My granny gave me this book and she said there were as many stories in it as there are stars in the sky."

"That book isn't nearly big enough to hold millions of stories," Juno grumped.

Billy grinned at her. "You *do* know that Cherry's auntie's book is magic, don't you?"

Cherry was waiting now with her book on her knee. Her eyes had a faraway look, and the fairytale shimmer that Mia had noticed, suddenly seemed brighter. When she looked at Cherry now, Mia totally believed that her great, great, great auntie had been a storyteller princess.

Cherry opened the book and for a puzzling moment Mia was looking at empty pages. Then a printed title appeared – *The Boy who Talked to Birds*. And then the blank pages filled with words.

Mia felt tiny prickles of excitement as Cherry read, "Once upon a time."

The bedroom filled with the sounds of the forest. Twigs cracked, wood pigeons cooed and water trickled over stones. Then Mia blinked

as she found herself looking *through* the pages into another world!

Next minute, Mia gasped as she felt a part of her slip *inside* the magic book. She was still in the bedroom, sitting squashed up to Juno on Cherry's bed. But part of her could smell damp mossy smells and feel the sun on her face. Part of her was *inside* the story!

Beside Mia, Billy and Juno gasped at the same moment. They were inside the story too. For a second, Mia panicked. Suppose they couldn't get back to the real world? Then she thought: 'We can't get lost. We're with Cherry Green, the Story Queen!'

Like a shining thread, Cherry's voice led them deeper and deeper into the forest. Soon they saw a boy walking all alone. He was homeless and hungry. His parents had thrown him out in disgrace. His mother and father had sent him to a very expensive teacher in the hope that he would become rich and clever. But then he came home again and they asked him what he'd learned. "I understand what the birds say when they sing," he told them. His parents were disgusted. "You stupid boy! Who *cares* what birds sing about?" they said. And they told him to leave their house and never come back.

The boy walked for days until he came to the edge of a large and beautiful city. In the city, the birds were acting very oddly. Blackbirds, thrushes, sparrows, woodpeckers were all flying in and out of the houses, beating their wings against the windows, crying out in their wild bird voices, trying to make the humans understand what they had to say.

The boy instantly understood that the birds were crying out a warning: *"Soldiers are coming! Run and tell the king!"*

He called back to the birds in their own language. "I'll tell the king but I'm just a boy, he might not believe me!"

"Then we'll come with you," cried the birds.

Later that day, the king looked out of his window and was amazed to see a boy walk through the palace gates with a great cloud of birds flying over his head. "He must be a very powerful wizard," said the king and he hurried out to meet him.

The boy had come with the birds' warning just in time. The king listened to his tale, the invaders were driven away and the kingdom was saved. The strange boy who talked to birds, grew up to marry the king's daughter and become a great hero.

"*And they all lived happily ever after*," said Cherry's voice.

And in an instant Mia was back in the front bedroom with the others, rubbing her eyes and feeling as if she had been on a long and wonderful journey.

Billy gave a happy sigh. "That boy wasn't stupid. He was a hero."

"His parents got it so, *so* wrong!" Juno agreed. Mia could see she was still half inside the story. She seemed to have forgotten that she'd thought stories were useless.

"I liked how that boy had a diamond stud in his ear like me," Billy said.

"Did he? I didn't notice that," said Mia.

"No, he *totally* did," said Billy, yawning.

*

In the night Mia shot awake. She thought she'd heard the bedroom door open and close, but then she decided it was only part of her dream.

'I can't wait for Cherry to read us some more stories tomorrow,' she thought.

But when morning came, Cherry's book had vanished.

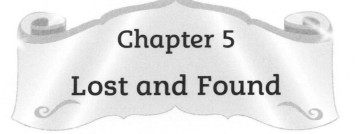

Chapter 5

Lost and Found

Before they went to sleep, Cherry had put her book away safe in its piece of carpet inside her bag. The thief had left the carpet behind on the landing.

Mia picked it up and stroked its glowing colours. The thief had to be Kyle. Who else would have taken Cherry's magic book?

Juno's eyes were full of angry tears. "I knew Kyle would try to get you back."

"It's OK, Juno," Cherry told her.

Juno was astonished. "Kyle stole your magic book and you say it's OK?"

"We could ask Mrs Turvey to search Kyle's room," Mia said.

Cherry shook her head. "I'm pretty sure Kyle will bring it back."

"And that makes it all right, does it?" Juno choked. "Sneaking into our room while we're asleep. Nicking your book out of your bag! I'm *ashamed* of him, I really am!"

Mia was ashamed of Kyle too. 'We never should have included him in our wish,' she thought. 'He doesn't deserve to live happily ever after.' She felt totally miserable.

Juno gave Cherry a strange look. "You *knew* Kyle was going to take it, didn't you?"

"I had a feeling that's what he'd do," Cherry said.

"Then why didn't you hide it?" Juno demanded.

"Because I knew he'd bring it back," said Cherry.

"But this is your magic book that's been in your family *forever!*" Juno said. "Kyle could throw it in a skip, or set it on fire. He's not a nice person, Cherry!"

"He'll bring it back," Cherry repeated.

Mia stared at her, astonished. It was almost like Cherry *trusted* Kyle, like she knew something about him they didn't.

At first it seemed that Cherry had got it wrong. There was no sign of Kyle at breakfast or lunch. He didn't turn up for tea either. Mia heard Mrs Turvey on the phone. "I've never known him miss a meal before," she was saying. "He's a good boy underneath."

Mia found herself hoping he wouldn't come back. Life was much more peaceful without Kyle making trouble for everyone.

They were in their bedroom playing a loud game of dominoes with Billy, when the door was suddenly flung open and Kyle strode in.

"What are you playing at, tricking little kids?" Kyle demanded. He shoved Cherry's book right under her nose. He had brought it back, just like Cherry said he would, but he looked as if he wanted to hit someone.

"Who did I trick?" Cherry asked.

"Everybody in this house! Always going on about story queens and happy endings. It's blank!" Kyle flicked through the pages. "Blank, blank, blank. No story. No happy ending, Just BLANK!"

"It does seem that way, I know – " Cherry started

"Because it *is* that way," Kyle yelled.

Cherry stood up so they were face to face. She didn't get angry or upset. She didn't even raise her voice. "Listen, Kyle, you can steal my auntie's book, but you can't steal the stories inside. Magic doesn't work like that."

"Stop going on about magic, will you! It's all just *tricks*!" Kyle almost threw the book at Cherry. Mia was shocked to see he had tears in his eyes. He was actually *upset*.

Mia pictured Kyle sneaking Cherry's book out of the house, to some patch of wasteland somewhere. She could see him opening it and then closing it and opening it again and again, hoping to find magic, hoping for a happy ending, but just finding more and more blank pages.

"Everyone at Mrs Turvey's wants to live happily ever after," Billy had said. But Mia had made up her mind that Kyle was different. Until this moment, she had never truly believed that this angry bad boy could share her own dreams and longings.

Kyle was half-way out of the room when Cherry called his name. "Thank you for bringing my auntie's book back," she said.

Kyle stopped in his tracks. Mia thought he was going to say something, but then he just slouched off to his room.

Minutes later two curly little heads appeared around the door – Riley and Rosie. "It's nearly our bedtime so we've come for our story," Rosie said to Cherry in a shy voice.

Cherry read them a little kids' story about a bunch of dim-witted animals who ran around telling everyone that the sky was falling in. Riley and Rosie were still only four years old so they thought it was perfectly normal to go inside a story and meet talking ducks and hens. They were totally spellbound.

When the twins had gone to bed, Juno said, "Hurray! Now let's have some serious story time!"

She went to shut the door but Cherry stopped her. "Leave it open just a crack," she said.

'So Kyle can listen,' Mia thought.

It was one of those late summer nights when it doesn't get dark till late. But by the time Cherry finished reading, the moon was rising over the rooftops and Billy had fallen fast asleep.

Mia gazed out at the night sky, but part of her was still inside a world of magical beasts, cruel stepmothers and flying carpets.

Cherry took out the piece of carpet and began to put her book away. All of a sudden Billy woke up. "Once upon a time, was that part of a real flying carpet?" he asked her dreamily.

Cherry put her fingers to her lips and gave him a very tiny nod, as if it was their secret.

Billy's eyes went huge. "It IS!"

"Come on, Billy, I'll take you to bed," Juno said.

Just then Mia heard a sudden scuffling sound on the landing. But when Juno opened the door there was nobody there.

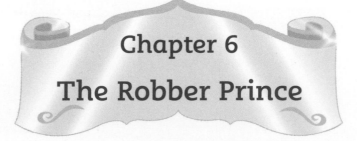

Chapter 6

The Robber Prince

It was Cherry's last night at Mrs Turvey's.

They had spent the day doing ordinary
fun summer things. They'd gone to the local
adventure playground then picked strawberries
at the city farm, and helped Mrs Turvey to
make strawberry shortcake for pudding. Kyle
had gone off for the afternoon with his mates.
He was home in time for tea, but he kept his
head down over his plate and gave "yes" and
"no" answers when anyone spoke to him.

When evening came, Cherry said, "How about we put heaps of pillows and cushions on the floor? That will be much more comfy."

When they'd finished arranging everything, she said, "Now my auntie would really feel at home! It's just like Persia in the olden days!"

They settled down on their cushions. Billy leaned against Cherry and she began to read a story called *The Robber Prince*.

In a heartbeat, Mia had entered the world of the story. An evil wizard wanted revenge on the king and queen, so he stole their baby son out of his cradle. Then he left the crying newborn baby on a heap of dried leaves in the forest, all alone. Night came. Mia gasped with fright as she saw several pairs of huge yellow eyes glowing in the dark. It was a pack of hungry wolves!

Mia heard them panting. She smelled their hot meaty breath as they padded closer and closer to the baby. Then at that exact moment she sensed Kyle in the doorway.

Part of Mia was in the story, sick with terror, watching the wolves sniff the little prince all over. Another part of her was watching Kyle. For the first time since she'd known him, his pale green eyes were still. *All* of Kyle was still. He was listening so hard to the story he had almost stopped breathing.

Kyle edged nearer and nearer. All at once he was inside the story with Mia and the others, watching amazed as a she-wolf washed the lost baby boy with her long pink tongue.

Time passed and winter came to the fairytale forest. The baby was a toddler now, rolling around in the snow with the wolf cubs. Suddenly a pistol shot rang out. The wolves fled. A band of rough-looking men appeared among the trees. They were robbers!

Cherry told them how the robbers took the little prince to their hideout in the mountains, where he grew up to be the biggest, boldest robber of them all. He had many adventures where he outsmarted his enemies with his robber's cunning. But somewhere deep inside the young man was still a prince and he had a good and noble heart. In his last and best adventure he defeated the wizard who had stolen him from the palace as a child. Then he went down to the castle dungeons and let out all the people the wizard had taken prisoner over the years.

When at last the story ended, Mia couldn't seem to move. Juno and Billy looked as if they were in a kind of dream. They had been abandoned in the forest, licked by a kind she-wolf, adopted by a band of robbers, and lived to defeat a wicked wizard. Now they were back in Mrs Turvey's front bedroom and it was almost dark.

Then Mia glanced at Kyle and was amazed to see the same dreamy look on his face. He took a deep breath as if he was coming back from somewhere far, far away.

Cherry was watching Kyle too. At last he looked up and met her eyes.

For a long moment nobody spoke. Then Kyle said shyly, "How about reading us one of those stories that your auntie told that bonkers king?"

Mia saw Juno give a happy little shiver as Cherry opened the book at a new story.

'Everyone's different now,' Mia thought. Cherry hadn't waved a wand over Mrs Turvey's house to make everyone live happily ever after. She had done something even more wonderful. She had turned four random foster kids into heroes. Together they had climbed glass mountains, outsmarted trolls and magic genies and they had come back stronger, braver,

changed. Even Kyle. Kyle wasn't angry Kyle any more – the stories had changed him, the same way they'd changed the scary king who married Cherry's auntie. Mia could see it in Kyle's eyes. He was a king's son who'd got lost, a robber prince, a bad boy hero with a heart.

It was Mia's turn to give a happy shiver as Cherry turned to a new page and said, "Once upon a time …"

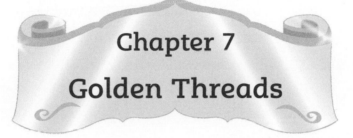

Chapter 7
Golden Threads

Mia never heard how the last story ended. She fell fast asleep on her cushions while Cherry was still reading.

She woke in the pale light of dawn to hear the sound of someone opening Mrs Turvey's gate. Mia flew to the window and was shocked to see Cherry walking down the street, carrying her patchwork bag over her arm.

She wanted to bang on the window so Cherry would turn round and see her looking.

She wanted to shout, "Come back!" Cherry had told them she was leaving after three days, but in her heart Mia had hoped she would stay. Not forever but as long as they needed her.

She felt Kyle come up behind her. "What's up?" Then he saw Cherry in the distance and his expression changed. "Oh, she's gone already."

"She never even said goodbye," Mia said in a shaky voice.

They stood there watching in silence until Cherry disappeared round a corner.

"I'm scared that I'll forget." Kyle's voice was shaky too. "Maybe in a few weeks, I'll think we made it all up." Like Mia, Kyle had fallen asleep in his clothes. He looked crumpled and tired and unhappy.

"I'm scared I'll forget too," Mia told him.

In stories, heroes came back from their adventures with pockets full of rubies, or a king's daughter for their bride. But real life wasn't like that, Mia thought sadly. In real life people didn't even always say goodbye.

"Where's Cherry?" Billy appeared beside them in his faded old PJs.

"What do you mean, 'where's Cherry?' She hasn't left already?" Juno scrambled up, rubbing her eyes.

Mia gave a sad nod. "Someone must have made a wish."

I'm only staying for three days. Like a magic whirlwind, Cherry Green, Story Queen, had come and gone.

"She's left us something to remember her by, though?" Billy was trying to make the best of things but his voice came out sounding very small.

"Cherry? All she had was her clothes and her book!" said Juno.

Billy suddenly dropped on his hands and knees. "She *did* leave us something!" He held up a fistful of golden threads, his eyes shining. "You know what these are? Magic threads from a real flying carpet. Cherry told me!"

Kyle sucked in a deep breath. For a moment it seemed like he was getting ready to make fun of Billy. Then he said, in a serious voice, "Threads from a flying carpet, yeah? That's got to be worth having!"

"Give them to me, Billy," Juno said suddenly. "I've got an idea. I'll need you to help, Mia! "

After breakfast Juno and Mia begged their foster mum for some coloured silk threads. Over the next few days the girls shut themselves away and worked on their secret project. While they worked they talked about Cherry, and how once they'd both felt like they were in the wrong story with no hope of a happy ending.

"It's funny because I don't feel like I'm in the wrong story any more," Mia said.

"Nor me," Juno agreed.

At last their secret project was finished.

One morning when it was just getting light, Juno and Mia woke up all the others and took them out into the misty garden. Here Juno handed over five friendship bracelets, one for every foster kid at Mrs Turvey's. She kept the sixth bracelet for herself.

Kyle stared at his bracelet. For a moment, his face was totally blank.

'He hates it,' Mia thought.

Then Kyle looked up with an amazed smile. "I'll never forget her now, will I?"

Mia almost fainted with relief. "That's what me and Juno thought!"

It had been tricky to do, but she was really proud of her and Juno's work. Each bracelet had a sparkling golden thread from a flying carpet. A thread of magic.

Our books are tested
for children and young people by
children and young people.

Thanks to everyone who consulted on
a manuscript for their time and effort in
helping us to make our books better
for our readers.